Peter Pan

by J. M. Barrie
adapted by Cathy East Dubowski
illustrated by Jean Zallinger

A Stepping Stone Book™ Classic

Random House 🏠 New York

Text copyright © 1991 by Random House, Inc.
Illustrations copyright © 1991 by Jean Zallinger.
Cover illustration copyright © 2003 by Anton Petrov.

All rights reserved under International and Pan-American Copyright Conventions.
Published in the United States by Random House Children's Books, a division of
Random House, Inc., New York, and simultaneously in Canada by Random House
of Canada Limited, Toronto. Originally published by Random House, Inc., in 1991.

www.randomhouse.com/kids

Library of Congress Cataloging-in-Publication Data:
Dubowski, Cathy East.
Peter Pan / by J. M. Barrie ; adapted by Cathy East Dubowski ; illustrated by Jean Zallinger.
  p. cm. — (A stepping stone book classic)
SUMMARY: A simplified retelling of the adventures of Peter Pan, the boy who would not
grow up.
ISBN 0-679-81044-7 (pbk.) — ISBN 0-679-91044-1 (lib. bdg.)
[1. Fantasy.] I. Zallinger, Jean, ill.   II. Barrie, J. M. (James Matthew), 1860–1937.
Peter Pan. III. Title. IV. Series. PZ7.D8544 Pe 2003 [Fic]—dc21 2002155168

Printed in the United States of America 25 24 23 22 21 20 19 18 17 16

RANDOM HOUSE and colophon are registered trademarks and A STEPPING STONE BOOK and
colophon are trademarks of Random House, Inc.

Contents

Chapter One

Peter Breaks Through

All children—except one—grow up. They begin to know it after they are two. And that was when Wendy Darling began to know it.

The Darlings lived in London at number 14. Wendy was the oldest. Then came John and little Michael. Mrs. Darling loved her children and wanted everything just so. But Mr. Darling was always worried about money. So the children had a nurse.

But the nurse was a huge dog named Nana.

Nana's kennel was in the night nursery. She awoke at the slightest cry. Nana was a treasure, as Mr. Darling well knew. But sometimes he worried that the neighbors talked. Even worse, he worried that Nana did not admire him enough. Being admired was very important to Mr. Darling.

The Darlings were a happy family. That is, until Peter Pan came.

Mrs. Darling first learned of Peter when she was tidying up her children's minds. All good mothers do this after their children go to sleep. It is quite like tidying up drawers. Mrs. Darling tucked the bad thoughts down at the bottom. She folded the beautiful thoughts right on top. Ready for her children to put on as soon as they awoke in the morning.

Have you ever seen a map of a child's mind? Each one is different. But all of them are very confusing. A child's mind is a Neverland. It is filled with skipping stones and chocolate pudding, verbs, and the first day of school. There are zigzag lines everywhere. Those are the roads on the island.

For the Neverland is always an island. It has caves and pirates and lagoons and mermaids. And children are always at play on those magic shores.

Mostly Mrs. Darling did not worry about what she found in her children's minds. But then she came across the word *Peter*.

"Who is Peter?" Mrs. Darling asked Wendy the next day.

"You know, Mother," said Wendy. "Peter Pan."

At first Mrs. Darling did not know. Then she remembered a Peter who was said to live among the fairies. Perhaps she had even believed in him as a child. But now she was married and full of sense. So Mrs. Darling had put Peter out of her mind.

A few nights later there were leaves by the nursery window. "I do believe that Peter tracked them in," said Wendy.

Mrs. Darling did not know what to think. The nursery was three stories up! Thirty feet from the ground and no way to climb up!

Mrs. Darling told Mr. Darling.

"Oh, it is just some nonsense Nana has put in their heads," said Mr.

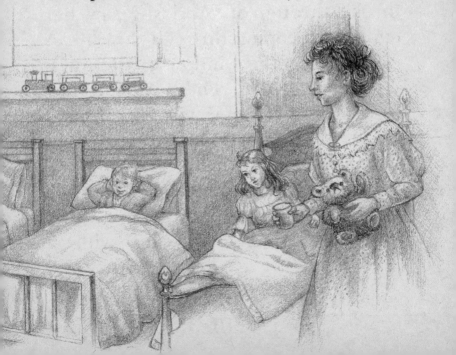

Darling. "Leave it alone and it will blow over."

But of course, it did not blow over.

The next evening was Nana's night off. Mrs. Darling tucked the children into bed. Then she sat by the fire in the nursery to sew. Soon she fell asleep.

But her dreams were troubled. She dreamed that the Neverland came too near. She dreamed that a strange boy broke through it. And she saw her children peeping through the gap.

Suddenly the window of the nursery blew open. There was a boy dressed in a suit of leaves. He dropped to the floor like a cat. A strange light no bigger than your fist flew with him. It twinkled and darted about the room like a living thing.

Mrs. Darling woke up with a

scream. She knew at once that the boy was Peter Pan. He still had all his baby teeth.

Nana had just come home. The scream brought her rushing into the nursery. She sprang at the boy. But he leapt through the open window.

Mrs. Darling screamed again. Surely the poor boy had fallen to his death! She ran to the street. But his body was not there. She looked up into the dark night sky. All she saw was what looked like a shooting star.

But Nana had caught something in her mouth. It was the boy's shadow!

Nana knew the boy would come back for it. And she did not want him to upset the children. So she hung the shadow out the window. He could get it when he pleased and be on his way.

But Mrs. Darling would not have

that. It looked as if washing was hanging out the front window. What would the neighbors think!

Quickly Mrs. Darling rolled up the shadow. Then she hid it in a drawer. She would have to tell Mr. Darling. But how?

Chapter Two

The Children Are Left Unguarded

One night the Darlings were getting ready for a dinner party. Mrs. Darling went into the nursery to show Wendy her new gown.

Suddenly Mr. Darling rushed in. "This tie won't tie!" he thundered.

Then Nana brushed against him. She got hairs on his new trousers. On top of everything, Michael would not take his medicine.

"I always took my medicine without a fuss when I was a boy," said Mr. Darling. "Why, I would take my own medicine now to show you. But I've lost the bottle." In fact, Mr. Darling had hidden it.

"I know where it is!" cried Wendy. She quickly brought him the bottle. "Why don't you and Michael take your medicine together?"

Mr. Darling did not like that idea one bit. But what could he do?

Wendy counted, "One, two, three!" Michael took his medicine. But Mr. Darling hid his behind his back!

"Oh, Father!" cried Wendy.

The children stared as if they no longer admired him. Even Mrs. Darling shook her head.

Mr. Darling was embarrassed. Perhaps a good joke would make them respect him again. "Look!" he said. "I'll pour my medicine into Nana's milk. Won't that be funny?"

Mr. Darling called Nana to her bowl. The children tried to stop her. But Nana began to drink the milk.

Suddenly she stopped. She looked up at Mr. Darling with tears in her eyes. Then she crept into her kennel.

The poor dog! Mrs. Darling and the children ran to her side. Mr. Darling completely lost his temper.

"I will not allow that animal to rule my nursery any longer!" he shouted. "The proper place for a dog is in the yard!"

The children wept. Nana begged. But Mr. Darling wanted to show them who was master. He dragged Nana outside and chained her in the yard.

Mrs. Darling put the children to

bed. They could hear Nana barking
out in the cold.

Soon Mr. and Mrs. Darling stepped
out into the snowy night. Their party
was at number 27, just a few houses
down. The stars watched till the door
shut behind them. Then the smallest
of the stars cried:

"Now, Peter!"

Chapter Three

Come Away! Come Away!

A twinkling light darted into the nursery. It was a tiny fairy called Tinker Bell.

Then the window blew open. Peter Pan dropped to the floor.

"Tink!" he whispered. "Do you know where they've put my shadow?"

"In the chest of drawers!" she said. The fairy's language was like the tinkling of golden bells.

Peter jumped at the drawers. He dug through the nicely folded things.

He tossed them over his shoulder left and right. There was his shadow! He slammed the drawer. And shut Tinker Bell inside!

Peter was surprised. Why didn't his shadow jump right back on him? He tried to stick it on with a bar of soap. But that didn't work, either. Peter flopped to the floor and cried.

The sound of his crying woke Wendy. "Boy," she said politely. "Why are you crying?"

Peter sprang to his feet. "Who are you?"

"I am Wendy Moira Angela Darling," she said.

"I am Peter Pan," said the boy. "I was crying because my shadow won't stick. But I wasn't really crying."

Wendy knew at once what to do. She took out her needle and thread.

Then she sewed the shadow back on.

"Oh, Wendy!" crowed Peter. "One girl is worth twenty boys!"

"Really, Peter?" Wendy was so pleased, she offered to give him a kiss.

Peter stuck out his hand. He clearly didn't know what a kiss was! Wendy did not want to hurt his feelings. So she gave him her thimble.

"Now shall I give you a kiss, too?" he asked.

"If you please," said Wendy. Peter dropped an acorn button into her hand.

Wendy sighed. "I know what I'll do," she said. "I'll put your kiss on a chain. Then I can wear it around my neck." That seemed to please Peter.

"How old are you?" Wendy asked.

Peter frowned. "I don't know," he

said. He didn't like questions that he didn't know the answer to. "I ran away the day I was born."

"Really?!" said Wendy. "Why?"

"I heard my father and mother talking," said Peter. "They were planning what I would be when I became a man. But I don't want to grow up. I want to be a boy and have fun forever. So I ran away to live with the fairies."

"Oh, Peter!" cried Wendy. "Tell me about the fairies! Would you, please?"

Peter smiled. He knew all about that.

"Fairies began long ago," he said. "When the first baby laughed for the first time, its laugh broke into a thousand pieces. The pieces all went skipping about. Each piece became a fairy.

And that is how fairies began.

"There should be one for every girl and boy," he said.

"But sometimes a child says, 'I don't believe in fairies.' Each time one does, a fairy dies."

An angry shake of bells came from the chest of drawers. "Why, I must have shut Tinker Bell up in the drawer," said Peter.

He opened the drawer. The little fairy flew about the nursery. She was tinkling with fury.

"She's lovely!" cried Wendy.

"Tink," said Peter. "Would you like to be Wendy's fairy?"

Tinker Bell answered with an angry jangle.

Peter shook his head. "She is not very polite," he told Wendy. "She says you are an ugly girl. And she says that she is my fairy. But she knows she can't be *my* fairy. After all, I am a gentleman and she is a lady."

Tink flew off in a huff.

"Where do you live now?" Wendy asked.

"With the lost boys," said Peter. "Children who fall out of their carriages and are forgotten. I'm their captain."

"What fun!" cried Wendy.

"Yes," said Peter. "But we are very lonely. You see, we have no mothers. That's why I come to your window. To hear your mother tell stories. She was telling such a nice one. It was about a lady with a glass slipper."

"Oh, Cinderella!" said Wendy. "She and the prince live happily ever after."

Peter leapt to the window. "I must tell the other boys how it ended!"

"Peter!" Wendy cried. "I know lots of stories!"

Peter stopped on the sill. He had a greedy look in his eyes. He pulled Wendy toward the window. "Come away with me and tell the other boys, too!"

Wendy was frightened. "Let me go! I can't fly!"

"Come away with me and I'll teach you!" said Peter. "Wendy, there are mermaids there . . ."

"Really?" cried Wendy.

Peter knew he almost had her. "You could tuck us in at night and mend our clothes. You could be our mother."

That did it! Wendy ran to wake her

brothers. "Peter Pan has come. He's going to teach us to fly!"

John and Michael were up and ready in a second.

Peter blew fairy dust on them. "Wiggle your shoulders," he said. Soon they were all flying!

Nana was barking wildly down in the yard. At last she broke loose and ran down the street to number 27.

Mr. and Mrs. Darling rushed into the street. They looked up at the nursery window. It was filled with light. And they saw four flying shadows on the curtains!

The Darlings might have reached the nursery in time. But the stars were watching. A young one blew open the window. "Hurry, Peter!" it cried.

Nana and the Darlings ran inside and up the stairs. They flung open

the door to the nursery. But it was
too late.

The children were gone.

Chapter Four

The Flight

"Second to the right, and straight on until morning."

That was the way to the Neverland, Peter said. But even birds with maps could not have found it that way. For you see, Peter just said whatever came into his head.

Wendy, Michael, and John flew through the air in their nightclothes. They followed Peter without question. Sometimes it was dark. Sometimes it was light. And now they were flying far out over the sea.

How long had they been gone? The children could not tell for sure.

Finally Peter stopped. "There it is," he said.

The children stood on tiptoe in the air to see. A million golden arrows pointed toward an island. It seemed so familiar. Like home after a long vacation.

They flew toward the island. Then something seemed to push against them. The golden arrows disappeared. The island grew dark and unfriendly.

"The pirates have spotted us," Peter said.

"They'll see Tinker Bell's light!" cried Wendy. "Tell her to put it out."

"She can't," said Peter. "It only goes out when she falls asleep."

But John had brought his tall black hat. Peter hid the fairy in that.

Just then the pirates fired their cannon into the sky. The blast scattered the children across the darkness. Wendy found herself alone with Tink.

It is important to understand one thing. Fairies are very small. They have room for only one feeling at a

time. Sometimes it is all good. Sometimes it is all *bad*.

Tinker Bell was so jealous of
Wendy! She was filled with bad hate-
ful feeling. From the tips of her wings
to the tips of her toes!

Tinker Bell darted this way and
that. "Come with me to safety," she
seemed to say.

Wendy did not know that Tinker
Bell hated her. So she followed the
little fairy.

Chapter Five

The Island Comes True

Down on the island the Neverland came to life.

The lost boys were looking for Peter. The pirates were looking for the lost boys. And the Indians were looking for the pirates. But they were all going at the same speed. So they just kept going around and around the island.

The boys were dressed in animal skins. There was Tootles, Nibs, Slightly, Curly, and the Twins. They lived in a home under the ground. Each boy had his very own hollow tree for a secret entrance. That is how they hid from the pirates.

"Look!" cried Nibs. "There's Tinker Bell!"

The boys looked into the sky. Tink flew around what looked like a great white bird. But it was really Wendy in her long white nightgown.

"Hurry!" shouted Tink. "Peter wants you to shoot the Wendy."

The boys never questioned Peter's orders. Tootles raised his bow and arrow and fired.

The arrow struck Wendy's chest. She fluttered to the ground.

A terrible silence fell upon the woods. The lost boys crowded around Wendy.

"This is no bird," said Slightly. He

spoke in a scared voice. "I think it must be a lady!"

Suddenly they heard Peter crow to signal his return. "Great news, boys!" he cried as he dropped to the ground. "I have brought you a mother!"

The boys shook with fear.

"She is dead!" Tootles cried. "From my arrow."

Peter knelt by Wendy's body.

"Look," he said. "The arrow struck this acorn button. It's my kiss. It saved her life!"

Golden bells shook above them. Tinker Bell was crying. She did not want Wendy to live. Then the boys told Peter what Tinker Bell had done.

"Tink!" cried Peter. "I am your friend no more! Leave me for ever!" Then he felt Wendy's hand upon his arm. "All right, not for ever," Peter said. "But for a whole week!"

Then he turned back to Wendy. They were afraid to move her. But they could not leave her outside. "Let's build a house around her!" said Peter.

"If only we knew what kind of house she likes best," said Tootles.

Wendy's eyes were still closed. But she suddenly began to sing:

I wish I had a pretty house,
The littlest ever seen,
With funny little red walls
And roof of mossy green.

The boys were delighted. They chopped down trees. They brought things from their underground houses. They put John's hat on top for a chimney. At last they were finished. Peter wiped his feet and knocked at the front door.

Wendy opened it. The lost boys fell to their knees. "Oh, Wendy lady, be our mother," they begged.

"I am just a little girl," said Wendy. "But I will do my best. Come inside then, you naughty children. I have just enough time to finish the story of Cinderella. Then I will put you all to bed."

Chapter Six
Captain Hook

The pirates still crept through the night forest. What an evil gang they were! Yet even they trembled before their leader—the black-hearted Captain James Hook.

Hook dressed in velvet and lace. He wore his hair in long black curls. And he had the speech and manners of a perfect gentleman. Except when he was running you through with his sword! Then his blue eyes burned

with two red spots. But that was not the worst of it.

In place of his right hand was an iron hook.

The captain paused among the trees and sighed. Such a beautiful night! Suddenly he felt like talking.

"I know what I'd do if I were a mother," Hook told his man Smee. "I would pray that my children be born with a hook." Yet it was the hook that made him hate Peter.

"It was Pan who cut off my arm," Hook explained. "Then he fed it to a crocodile. The croc found me *delicious*. And it has followed me ever since."

"In a way it's a compliment," said Smee.

"I want no such compliments!" barked Hook. "I want Peter Pan. He's the one who gave the croc its taste for me!"

Hook sat down on a large mushroom. "That crocodile would have had me by now. But it swallowed a clock. Now it ticks! That warns me to run away."

"Some day the clock will run down," said Smee.

"Aye, that's the fear that haunts me," said Hook. "And it's all Pan's doing! I've waited long enough. I want to shake his hand with *this*!" He sliced the air with the deadly hook.

Suddenly the captain jumped up. "Odds bobs, hammer and tongs! This mushroom is hot!"

Hook and Smee looked at the thing. They pulled it loose. Smoke rose in the air. "A chimney!" they exclaimed. Then something else came out.

The chatter of boys.

The pirates had found the chimney to the home under the ground!

Wendy had put the boys to bed. But they were far too excited to sleep.

The captain's lips curled into a wicked smile. "Back to the ship! We'll cook up a large rich cake. With thick green sugar on it! Then we'll leave it here where the boys will find it."

He giggled. "They have no mother. Don't you see? They won't know how dangerous it is to eat rich damp cake. They'll gobble it up. And die!" Hook shook with laughter.

Tick tick tick tick.

"The crocodile!" gasped Hook. The captain ran off with his long curls flying. Smee was close behind.

Chapter Seven

The Home Under the Ground

Next day Peter measured Wendy, John, and Michael. He found hollow trees for them. Soon they could go up and down as easily as buckets in a well. How they loved it!

The home under the ground was one large room. Mushrooms grew out of the floor for stools.

A Never tree tried to grow in the middle of the room. But each morning they sawed it down to the floor. That left more room to play. By suppertime the stump had grown two feet. The boys laid a door on top. It made a perfect table! Then they chopped it down again when they were ready to play.

The boys all slept in one huge bed. But Wendy made Michael sleep in a basket. Michael had to be the baby.

Tinker Bell lived in a hole in the wall. It had tiny furniture. The bedspread was made of flowers.

Wendy stayed very busy looking after the boys. She rarely went above ground. The cooking kept her nose to the pot. Even if sometimes the pot was empty. For she never knew if the food would be real or make-believe. That was up to Peter. Make-believe was so real to him. He could eat a pretend meal and grow fat before your eyes.

The home had a huge fireplace where Wendy hung the wash to dry. And she never ran out of mending to do. But she saved it until the boys were asleep.

One night she sat in a rocker before the fire.

"At last!" she said. "A moment to myself."

She looked at her mending basket and sighed. It was full of socks. And every sock had a hole in the toe!

"Sometimes I think children are more trouble than they're worth!" she said. But then she smiled. For Wendy had never been happier in her life!

Weeks went by. Sometimes Wendy thought of home and her dear mother and father. But John had trouble remembering. And as for Michael! He already believed that Wendy really was his mother!

Chapter Eight

The Mermaids' Lagoon

Imagine a lagoon that sparkles with the colors of the rainbow. Where the singing of mermaids fills the air. That was the lagoon of the Neverland. It was the children's favorite place to stay.

Wendy longed to talk to the mermaids. But they were friendly only to Peter. They dived into the water whenever she came near. They splashed her with their tails. Wendy feared they did it on purpose.

One day the children had a picnic on Marooners' Rock. Wendy settled them down for a short nap after lunch. Then she took up her pile of mending.

Slowly a change came over the lagoon. The sun slipped away. Dark shadows stole across the water.

Peter could sniff danger even in his sleep. He sprang awake. "Pirates!" he cried. He quickly woke the others and ordered them to dive.

Wendy and Peter watched a rowboat draw up to Marooners' Rock. The pirates Starkey and Smee had a prisoner.

"That's Tiger Lily, daughter of the Indian chief," Peter whispered.

The Indian princess was tied up. The pirates shoved her onto the rock. She would surely drown when the tide rose! But Tiger Lily showed no fear.

Peter could have waited until the pirates left to save Tiger Lily. But that was not Peter's way.

"Ahoy, there!" he called out in the darkness of the afternoon. His voice sounded just like Hook's! "Set her free—or you'll feel my hook!"

The pirates dared not question their captain's voice. They untied Tiger Lily, and she quickly swam away.

Peter felt so clever that he was about to crow. But Wendy clapped her hand over his mouth.

"Ahoy, there!" sounded Hook's voice again. "Help me into the blasted boat!"

But this time it was not Peter. It was the real James Hook!

"Captain!" said Smee. "Is all well?"

"Our plans are ruined!" Hook moaned. "The lost boys have found a mother!"

"Oh, evil day!" said Starkey.

"Captain," said Smee. "Why not kidnap the boys' mother? We could make her be our mother instead."

Hook's eyes lit up. "A treasure of an idea! We can make her boys walk the plank!"

Suddenly the captain remembered Tiger Lily.

"Where is the Indian princess?" he demanded.

"We let her go," said Starkey, smiling with satisfaction.

"Just like you ordered," said Smee.

"What!" Hook thundered. "I gave no such order!"

But Hook saw they believed their

words. Someone—or some *thing*—had spoken to them. He shivered and peered into the heavens.

"Spirit that haunts this dark lagoon. Do you hear me?" Hook asked.

Peter answered in a perfect imitation of Hook's voice: "Odds bobs, hammer and tongs. I hear you!"

The pirates froze in terror.

"Who are you?" Hook demanded. "Speak!"

"I am James Hook," said the voice. "Captain of the *Jolly Roger*."

"Brimstone and gall!" said Hook. "Then who am I?"

"A codfish!" said the voice.

Hook saw his men draw back. They looked as if they no longer admired him! It broke his heart.

"Do you have another voice?" Hook asked the voice. "Another name?"

"Yes!" crowed the voice. "I am Peter Pan!"

"Pan!" Hook nearly choked with anger. "Into the water, Smee!" he roared. "Take him, dead or alive!"

The water was soon churning with boys and pirates.

At last Hook dragged himself back to the rock. He needed to catch his breath. Peter was crawling up the opposite side. Neither knew the other was there. Both reached for a hold— and their hands touched.

Peter grabbed a knife from Hook's belt. He aimed the blade at the captain's heart.

But then Peter stopped. He saw that he was higher up on the rock than Hook. Peter hated a fight that was not fair.

He started to help the captain up.

But Hook never played fair. He bit Peter's hand!

The pain meant nothing to Peter. But the cheating dazed him. It made him quite helpless!

Hook took his chance. He slashed twice at the boy with his hook. Then a sound stilled his arm.

Tick tick tick tick!

"The crocodile!" Hook cried out in fear. Then he swam like a fish for the *Jolly Roger*.

Chapter Nine
The Never Bird

Peter and Wendy lay on Marooner's Rock. The water was rising. But Wendy had fainted. And Peter was too weak to fly.

Just then something brushed Peter's cheek. It was the tail of a lost kite.

Peter woke Wendy. "It can carry only one of us," he said. He tied the kite tail around her waist.

"Shouldn't we draw straws?" called Wendy. But the kite was already lifting her into the sky.

Peter was alone. The rock grew smaller as the water rose. Soon it would be completely under water.

A wave of fear ran through Peter. But then he smiled. A drum began to beat within him. And the drum seemed to say: "To die will be an awfully big adventure!"

Peter waited bravely, staring at the sea.

He thought he saw a piece of paper floating on the water. It seemed to fight the tide. Peter clapped for the paper. He always cheered for the weaker side.

But it was not a piece of paper at all. It was the Never bird floating in her nest.

Once the bird and her nest had fallen into the lagoon. Peter had given orders that she not be harmed. Now she always made her nest upon the water.

The Never bird saw that Peter was in trouble. Now it was her turn to help him. Her nest was filled with eggs. But she bravely offered it to Peter.

Peter had an idea. Smee had left his hat on the rock. Now Peter laid the eggs in the hat. Then he set it upon the waters. It floated beautifully.

Then Peter sailed away in the nest. When he reached land, he left it where the Never bird could find it. But she liked the hat much better. To this day all Never birds build their nests in the shape of a pirate hat.

At last Peter reached the home under the ground. Everyone was safe. Each had an adventure to tell. But the biggest adventure of all was that they

had stayed up hours past bedtime.

"To bed, to bed," Wendy said at last.
And the boys gratefully obeyed.

Chapter Ten
Wendy's Story

Peter had saved Tiger Lily. Now there was nothing the Indians would not do for Peter. They stood guard above his underground home.

Down below the lost boys were having their make-believe supper. Peter and Wendy sat before the fire. They pretended to be the mother and father.

Then Peter blinked his eyes. "It is only make-believe. Isn't it, Wendy? That I am their father?"

Wendy sighed. "Yes. Only make-believe."

Soon it was bedtime. The lost boys asked for their favorite story. The one that Peter hated.

"There once was a gentleman," Wendy began. "His name was Mr. Darling. His wife was Mrs. Darling."

"I knew them!" said John.

"I think I knew them. . . . " said Michael.

"They had three children," Wendy went on. "And a faithful nurse named Nana. But Mr. Darling was angry with Nana. He chained her in the yard. Then the children flew away to the Neverland."

"What a good story!" said the First Twin.

"But think of the poor parents," said Wendy.

"Did they ever go back?" asked the Second Twin.

"Yes," said Wendy. "After many years. Their mother loved them very much. And she always left the window open. All they had to do was fly right in."

Peter hissed. "You are wrong about mothers, Wendy." The boys looked startled.

"Long ago I thought like you," said Peter. "I thought my mother would keep my window open forever. So I stayed away for many months. Then I flew back. The window was locked. Another boy was in my bed."

This may have been true. It may have been make-believe. It was hard to tell with Peter. But Peter believed it was true. The story frightened the children.

"Wendy!" cried John. "Let's go home!"

"Of course," said Wendy. "At once."

Peter was stung! Leave it to grown-ups to spoil all the fun! But he would show Wendy! He would act as if he didn't care.

But the boys did not want to lose their mother.

"We won't let you go!" said one.

"Let's keep her prisoner!" cried another.

The boys looked so sad. Wendy had an idea. "Why not come with us? My father and mother can adopt you." She looked at Peter. She was mostly asking him.

"Can we, Peter?" the boys asked.

"All right," said Peter. But Wendy saw the look on Peter's face. Her heart sank.

"Peter," she said, shaking. "Get your things!"

"No," said Peter. "I am not going with you."

"But we could find your mother," Wendy said.

"No," said Peter. "I just want to be a little boy and have fun forever."

"Will you remember to take your medicine?" Wendy asked.

"Yes," he answered.

There seemed nothing more for Wendy to say.

Just then the ground above them shook. The air filled with the battle cry of pirates and Indians!

Wendy fell to her knees. She put her arms around the boys. Peter drew his sword.

But the battle above ground was

over quickly. Hook and his pirates had cheated. They had surprised the Indians. They had attacked in the dark! And they had won. Hook had Peter cornered!

Peter Pan was so small a boy for Captain Hook to hate so much. True, Peter had thrown Hook's arm to the crocodile. But that hardly seemed enough.

The truth was that Hook simply could not bear the sound of Peter crowing. It got on his nerves. It made his hook twitch. It worried him like a bug.

Hook tiptoed to a tree and listened for sounds from below. He heard Peter talking.

"Let's listen," Peter said. "The Indians always beat their tom-toms

when they win. That is their victory sign."

Hook whispered to Smee. Smee smiled a wicked smile. Then he began to beat the drum.

"The tom-tom!" they heard Peter cry. "The Indians have won!"

The children cheered. It was safe to go up!

Above them the pirates waited.

Chapter Eleven

Do You Believe in Fairies?

The pirates easily caught the children as they came up their trees. Then they carried them off to the *Jolly Roger*.

But Captain Hook had to go underground to find Peter. Carefully he squeezed down a hollow tree.

Peter was sleeping. His medicine was still in the cup. The captain grinned in the dark.

Hook always carried a small bottle

of yellow poison. Now he put five drops into Peter's medicine. Then he wormed his way back up the tree.

It was nearly ten o'clock when Tink woke Peter. "The pirates have captured Wendy and the boys!" she cried.

Peter's heart bobbed in his chest. Wendy! Tied up on the dirty pirate ship! Wendy who loved everything just so!

"I'll save her!" Peter cried. Then he remembered something. He knew it would please Wendy if he took his medicine.

He reached for the cup.

"No!" cried Tinker Bell. There was no time for words. She dashed in front of his lips and drained the cup.

"It was poisoned, Peter," she said. "And now I am going to die."

Her light was already fading. Soon it would go out. Then she would be gone forever.

Tinker Bell spoke softly now. Peter could barely hear. "Perhaps I could get well again," she whispered. "If only children believed in fairies . . ."

Peter flung out his arms. He spoke to children everywhere who might be dreaming of the Neverland:

"Do you believe?" he cried. "Do you!
Then clap your hands!"

Some children just turned over in their sleep. A few of the little beasts hissed. But many children clapped!

Then suddenly all of the clapping stopped. Mothers everywhere had rushed in to see what was wrong.

But it was enough. Tink was saved!

"And now to save Wendy!" Peter cried.

The moon was riding in a cloudy heaven. Peter stole through the forest. Once he saw the crocodile pass him. It didn't make a sound.

Peter was bursting with happiness. Tink was alive. And he was off on another adventure.

To save Wendy from Captain Hook!

Chapter Twelve
The Pirate Ship

The *Jolly Roger* lay wrapped in a blanket of darkness. Wendy was tied to the mast. The lost boys were about to walk the plank.

Wendy hated the pirates. The boys could not help but admire them a little. But all Wendy saw was how mean and messy they were. The ship had not been scrubbed for years.

"So, my beauty," Hook said. "Are you ready to see your boys walk the plank?" Suddenly he froze.

Tick tick tick tick tick tick.

Hook fell in a heap. His hook hung helpless in the air. "Hide me!" he gasped.

The pirates crowded around their captain. The boys rushed to the ship's side to see the crocodile. But it was not the crocodile.

It was Peter Pan!

Remember how the crocodile had passed Peter in the forest? Without a sound. The crocodile had stopped ticking. The clock inside had finally run down.

So Peter began to tick. At first it was just to scare the beasts in the night. Then he reached the *Jolly Roger.* And he saw that it frightened the pirates.

Peter ticked as he slipped on board.

He ticked as he hid in the cabin. Then he stopped ticking.

"Captain—the crocodile's gone!" said Smee.

Slowly Hook raised his head to listen. It was true. The ticking had stopped.

"Then here's to Johnny Plank!" he cried. His hatred for the boys was doubled now. For they had seen him shake in fear.

A shriek came from the cabin.

"Jukes," said Hook. "Find out what that was."

Jukes went into the cabin. But he did not come out. Cecco went in after him. There were terrible shrieks. But he did not come out, either.

"Drive the boys into the cabin," ordered Hook. "Maybe they will all kill each other."

The boys pretended to be afraid. The pirates shoved them into the cabin and shut the door.

Of course, only Peter was inside. He smiled and gave them weapons.

"Hide yourselves now," Peter whispered. "But stand ready for my call. I am going to free Wendy."

Quietly he snuck up and untied her. "Hide with the others," he whispered. "Hurry!"

Then he wrapped himself in Wendy's cloak. He would pretend to be Wendy. "Hook or me this time!" he swore.

Hook had decided there was bad luck on board. And he had decided the bad luck was Wendy!

"Throw her overboard!" Hook ordered. "Then all our troubles will be over!"

Peter hid his face. The pirates

crowded around the mast. "No one can save you now!" one shouted.

Peter spoke in a voice like Wendy's: "There's one who can."

"Who?!" said Hook.

"Peter Pan!" Peter flung off Wendy's cloak and crowed.

"So!" said Hook. "This is all your doing!"

"Aye, James Hook," Peter said with pride.

"Foolish boy," spat Hook. "Prepare to meet your doom."

Peter was a master with the sword.

But so was Hook. They fought each other with skill and passion.

At last Hook was cornered. He lashed out at the boy with his iron hook. But Peter lunged. His sword pierced the captain's ribs. Hook dropped his sword. The captain was at Peter's mercy.

"Now!" cried the lost boys.

However, Peter waited. The fight must be fair. And it must be fair to the finish.

James Hook took up his sword again. But he fought without hope. Escape was now his only chance. He backed up to the side of the boat. Then he threw himself into the sea.

He did not know that the silent crocodile had been drawn to Peter's ticking. That he had followed the boy.

That he waited below with hungry jaws.

And that was the end of Captain Hook.

The battle was over. But it was half past one in the morning! Wendy tucked the boys into the pirates' bunks. All but Peter. He had to strut up and down the deck for a while. Then he, too, fell asleep.

Peter had bad dreams that night. He cried in his sleep. Wendy held him tight.

The next morning the boys put on pirates' clothes. Captain Peter took the wheel and turned the ship toward the mainland.

He was taking Wendy home.

Chapter Thirteen

The Return Home

Peter had been wrong about mothers. At least, he was wrong about Mrs. Darling. She was waiting back in London at number 14. And she always kept the window open.

Mr. Darling blamed himself for the children's leaving. He swore he would live in Nana's kennel until they came home. He even went to work in the cage! His carriage ride to the office often drew quite a crowd.

One night Mr. Darling lay curled

up in the kennel. "Won't you play me to sleep on the nursery piano?" he asked his wife. "And shut that window," he added quite thoughtlessly. "I feel a draft."

"Oh, George!" cried Mrs. Darling. "Never ask me to do that. The window must always be left open for the children. Always."

Mr. Darling begged her pardon. Then Mrs. Darling went to the piano. She played until her husband fell asleep.

It would have been a perfect time for the children to come home! But Peter and Tink flew into the room instead. Peter had thought of a plan. And he had flown off ahead of the others.

"Quick, Tink," he whispered. "Close the window and lock it. Wendy will think her mother has locked her out. Then she will have to go back with me." He danced across the nursery floor shamelessly.

Then he heard Wendy's mother playing the piano in the next room. He did not know the tune. But he knew it was saying, "Come back, Wendy. Come back . . ."

Then the music stopped. Mrs. Darling laid her head on the piano. Her eyes filled with tears.

Peter frowned. Why won't she understand? he thought. We can't both have Wendy.

He stopped looking at her. He skipped about and made funny faces. But Peter felt Mrs. Darling inside him. She was knocking on the door of his heart.

"Oh, all right!" he said at last. He unlocked the window. "Come on, Tink! We don't want any silly mothers anyway."

So Wendy and John and Michael found the window open for them after all. Which was perhaps more than they deserved. They had been gone so long. And Michael had almost forgotten.

"I think I have been here before," he said.

"It's your home, silly," said John.

Wendy checked the kennel for

Nana. But instead she found her father fast asleep.

"Oh, dear!" said Wendy. "Maybe I don't remember the old life as well as I thought."

A chill fell upon the children. They decided to slip into their beds as if they had never been away.

Mrs. Darling came into the night nursery to check on her husband. The children waited for her cry of joy. But it did not come.

Mrs. Darling saw her children. But she could not believe they were *really* there. She had seen them there so often in her dreams.

"Mother!" cried Wendy.

"We're home!" cried John and Michael.

Mrs. Darling was still unsure. She reached out. Suddenly her arms were

filled with three very real children.

"George! George!" she cried. Mr. Darling woke up. Their reunion was a beautiful sight.

Only one strange boy was there to see it. He stared through the window. His life was filled with joys. Joys that other children could never know. But he had locked himself out from ever knowing joy like this.

Chapter Fourteen

When Wendy Grew Up

The lost boys stood before Mrs. Darling. They wished they weren't wearing pirate clothes. They said nothing. But their eyes asked her to have them.

"Of course I will have you," Mrs. Darling said. Poor Mr. Darling! Six boys would cost quite a lot!

"Don't worry, Father," said Wendy. "I always cut their hair myself."

"Then follow the leader," said Mr.

Darling. "I shall see if we can fit you into the drawing room."

Peter did not come in. But he didn't leave, either. He thought Wendy might want to say good-bye.

Mrs. Darling followed Wendy to the window. She was not about to lose her daughter again.

"Peter," said Mrs. Darling. "I would be glad to adopt you, too."

Peter thought about it. "Would you send me to school?"

"Yes."

"Then to an office?"

"Yes," said Mrs. Darling.

"Then my answer is no!" Peter cried. "No one is going to catch me and make me a man."

"But where will you live?"

"With Tink in the house we built for Wendy."

Mrs. Darling saw that Wendy longed to go. So she made a wise offer. "Wendy may come to visit you for one week each year. To do the spring cleaning."

That made Peter happy again. For he had no sense of time.

But Wendy knew spring would be long in coming. "You won't forget me, will you, Peter?" she asked.

But Peter Pan had already flown away.

All the lost boys went to school. Soon they saw how silly they had been. They never should have left the island. But what was done was done. Slowly their power to fly left them. And soon they no longer believed.

At the end of the first year Peter came back. Wendy hoped he did not notice how she had grown.

She had looked forward to talking with him about old times. But Peter had had new adventures. They seemed to have crowded the old ones out of his mind.

"Captain Hook?" he asked. "Who is that?"

"Don't you remember?" said Wendy. "You killed him and saved our lives."

"I forget them after I kill them," said Peter.

He could not remember Tinker Bell, either. Wendy was shocked.

It was painful for Wendy. But there were new adventures. And they had a lovely spring cleaning in the little house.

The next year Wendy waited. But Peter did not come.

Another year passed, and then he came again. He never even knew he had missed a year! That was the last time the girl Wendy ever saw Peter Pan.

You need not feel sorry for her, though. Wendy tried not to grow up for a long time. She wanted to please Peter. But in the end she grew up of her own free will. And she did it a day quicker than other girls.

Years went by. Wendy married and had a little girl. Her name was Jane. And she was born with a question on her lips. When Jane grew older, her questions were mostly about Peter Pan. Wendy told her all that she could remember.

Wendy's husband had bought number 14. So Jane slept in the same nursery her mother had.

It was a warm spring night. Jane was asleep in bed. Wendy sat by the fire mending a hole in a sock.

Suddenly she heard a crowing sound. The window blew open. Peter dropped to the floor.

He was the same as ever. He was a little boy with all his baby teeth. But Wendy was all grown up. She drew back into the shadows. She was afraid for him to see her.

"Hello, Wendy," said Peter. "Have you forgotten? It is spring-cleaning time."

"I can't come," she said softly. "I have forgotten how to fly."

"I'll teach you again—"

"Oh, Peter!" she said softly. "Don't waste the fairy dust on me." Wendy stood up.

And Peter saw. He cried out in pain.

"I am old, Peter," said Wendy. "I am ever so much more than twenty. I grew up long ago."

"You promised not to!" said Peter.

"I couldn't help it," she said. "I am married now. The girl in the bed is my daughter."

"It's not true!" said Peter. But he knew it was. He sat on the floor and began to cry.

His sobs woke Jane.

"Boy," she said. "Why are you crying?"

Peter sprang to his feet and bowed. "My name is Peter Pan. I came back for my mother. To take her to the Neverland for spring cleaning."

"Yes, I know," said Jane. "I've been waiting for you."

In the end Wendy let them fly away together. She stood at the window. She

watched until they were as small as stars. "If only I could go with you . . ." she whispered.

But that was years ago. Now Jane is grown up. She has a daughter named Margaret. Peter comes for Margaret every year. She tells him stories and does the spring cleaning. Only some years he forgets.

One day Margaret will have a daughter. And she will be Peter's mother in turn.

And that is how it will always be. As long as there are children who believe in the Neverland.

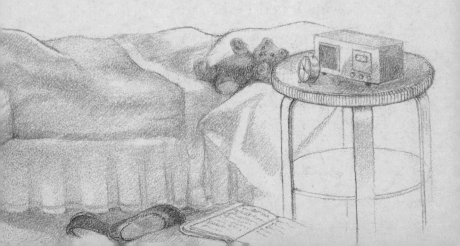

J. M. Barrie was born in Scotland in 1860. As a young boy, he loved stories about pirates and magic. He began writing plays as a teenager and grew up to be a successful playwright and author. Peter Pan first appeared as a character in three of Barrie's novels. But with the play *Peter Pan: or, the Boy Who Would Not Grow Up* Peter became a star. Barrie later retold the same story in a novel. This adaptation is based on the novel. Barrie wrote over forty plays and many novels. But *Peter Pan* is his one story that has passed the test of time.

Cathy East Dubowski is a freelance editor and writer. She has written several Step into Reading™ books and has also adapted *Black Beauty* and *A Little Princess* for this series. She lives in Chapel Hill, North Carolina, with her husband and children. She has always loved Peter Pan.

Jean Zallinger also illustrated *Oliver Twist* for this series. A careful observer of nature, Ms. Zallinger creates stamps that feature butterflies for the National Wildlife Federation. She lives in North Haven, Connecticut.